Pokémon World

Words and Music by John Loeffler (ASCAP)/John Siegler (BMI)

Rap:

So you wanna be a master of
POKÉMON
Understand the Secrets and
HAVE SOME FUN
So you wanna be a master of Pokémon
POKÉMON
Do you have the skills to be
NUMBER ONE?

Verse I:

I wanna take the ultimate step
Find the courage to be bold
To risk it all and not forget
The lessons that I hold

I wanna go where no one's been
Far beyond the crowd
Learn the way to take command
Use the power that's in my hand

Chorus:

We all live in a Pokémon World
I want to be the greatest master of them all
We all live in a Pokémon World
Put myself to the test
Be better than all the rest

Verse II:

Every day along the way
I will be prepared
With every challenge I will gain
Knowledge to be shared

In my heart there's no doubt
Of who I want to be
Right here standing strong
The greatest Master of Pokémon

Chorus:

Rap: You've got the power right in your hands

There are more books about Pokémon.

Collect them all!

coming soon

POKÉMON

THE JOHTO JOURNEYS

Teaming Up With Totodile

Adapted by Tracey West

SCHOLASTIC INC.
New York   Toronto   London   Auckland   Sydney
Mexico City   New Delhi   Hong Kong   Buenos Aires

JOHTO REGION

ISBN 0-439-29574-2

© 1995-2001 Nintendo, CREATURES, GAME FREAK.
TM & ® are trademarks of Nintendo.
Copyright © 2001 Nintendo.
All rights reserved. Published by Scholastic Inc.
SCHOLASTIC and associated logos are trademarks
and/or registered trademarks of Scholastic Inc.

12 11 10 9 8 7 6 5 4 3 2   1 2 3 4 5/6

Printed in the U.S.A.
First Scholastic printing, November 2001

Fighting Fire With Pokémon

"So your Tauros won a battle in Leaf Town," said Professor Oak. "Very impressive, Ash."

Ash Ketchum beamed into the videophone at Professor Oak's face. A Pokémon expert, Professor Oak had sent Ash and his friends on an errand to the Johto Region.

Ash, a Pokémon trainer, was happy to run the errand. It gave him a chance to catch new Pokémon, battle new trainers, and earn badges by battling the leaders of Pokémon gyms. He liked to report back to Professor Oak and let him know how he was doing. Today he and his friends had stopped at a Pokémon Center on the way to Goldenrod City.

"Tauros did a great job," Ash told the professor. "But I think I'll send it back to you. Taking care of Tauros is a lot of work. It's better off with you than it is on the road with me."

"No problem," replied the professor.

Ash took the red-and-white Poké Ball that contained Tauros and placed it on a transporter pad next to the videophone. Ash pressed a button, and the Poké Ball disappeared. It reappeared next to Professor Oak.

"I'll take good care of Tauros," said the professor. "Good luck with the rest of your Johto Journey."

The video screen went black.

A girl wearing blue shorts came into the room. Her orange hair bounced in a ponytail on top of her head.

"Ash, Nurse Joy is done examining your Pokémon," she said. "They're all fine."

Ash got up from his chair. His friend Misty had been traveling with him since he started

his journey. Ash's Pokémon were gathered around her. They all looked better after a little TLC from Nurse Joy, who ran the Pokémon Center.

Cyndaquil's blue skin looked shiny and clean. The little Pokémon with the long snout looked cute, but Ash knew it was also tough when hot flames shot out of its back.

Ash's Grass Pokémon, Bulbasaur and Chikorita, looked healthy, too. The green plant bulb on Bulbasaur's back looked ready to open up and lash out with a new attack. And Chikorita was shipshape, from the green leaf on top of its head to the green spots that ringed its neck.

Next, Ash checked out his Water Pokémon, Squirtle. Squirtle had a round shell on its back, and its big eyes shined brightly, as always.

Finally there was Pikachu. The little yellow Pokémon had round red cheeks, pointy ears, and a lightning-bolt-shaped tail. Pikachu looked ready to jolt any opponent with a shock of electricity.

"You guys look great," Ash told them.

Nurse Joy stepped into the room. "They're very healthy," she said. "You've been taking good care of them."

Ash's friend Brock, an older boy with dark brown hair, ran in behind Nurse Joy. "I make all their food, you know. I make sure they get the best nutrition."

"I can tell," Nurse Joy said. "Is there anything else I can do for you? I need to go check the Pokémon who will be competing in the Fire-and-Rescue Grand Prix."

"Is that some kind of Pokémon competition?" Ash asked. There was nothing he liked better than to see Pokémon in action.

Nurse Joy nodded. "It's being held in the stadium down the road."

Ash turned to his friends.

"Let me guess," Misty said. "You want to go check it out?"

"You bet," Ash said.

"Why not?" Misty said. "You need water to put out fire, so I bet there will be a lot of Water Pokémon there. And nobody loves Water Pokémon more than I do!"

They headed for the stadium. First, Ash

put Chikorita, Cyndaquil, and Bulbasaur back into their Poké Balls. Pikachu and Squirtle walked alongside Ash. Pikachu never traveled inside a Poké Ball, and Squirtle was interested to see the other Water Pokémon at the competition.

Misty carried one of her Pokémon in her arms. Tiny Togepi still wore the colorful eggshell from which it had hatched. Its little arms and legs poked out of the shell.

It was a short walk to the stadium. Next

door was a long building. As they passed the entrance, Ash noticed that it was filled with Pokémon and their trainers.

"The fire-fighting teams must be warming up before the competiton," Ash said. "Let's check it out."

Ash stepped into the building. The teams looked impressive. Ash saw a team of tough-looking Golduck lined up with a girl trainer. Dark feathers covered their bodies, and a jewel gleamed on each Golduck's head. In another corner, four chubby blue Marill practiced with their trainer.

"Ash Ketchum, is that you?"

Ash turned at the sound of the familiar voice. A tall young man wearing an orange jumpsuit held his hand out in greeting. Behind him were five Wartortle.

"Aidan, long time, no see," Ash said.

Squirtle walked up and greeted the Wartortle. Each Wartortle had long pointy ears and a curly blue tail. Two white fangs peeked out of each Wartortle's mouth. Ash wondered if his Squirtle would evolve into a Wartortle someday.

"Those Wartortle are in great shape," Brock remarked.

"What do you expect?" Misty said. "They're the famous Wartortle fighting team."

"Famous?" Brock asked.

"They're the best fire-fighting force in the Orange Islands," Misty explained. "Ash and I met Aidan when we were traveling there. Squirtle even helped the Wartortle put out a humongous fire."

"*Squirtle, Squirtle!*" Squirtle smiled at the Wartortle.

"Now we're entering the Fire-and-Rescue Grand Prix," Aidan said. "We're the returning champions, and I'm hoping for another win."

"Who do you think your biggest competition will be?" Misty asked.

"I'm not sure," Aidan said. "Those guys are supposed to be a tough team." Aidan pointed to a team of four Squirtle, which was shuffling into the practice building with worried expressions on their faces.

There was something familiar about those Squirtle, Ash thought, but he couldn't put his finger on it.

Squirtle's eyes opened wide when it saw the Squirtle team.

"*Squirtle!*" it said excitedly.

Suddenly, Ash knew what was so familiar about those Squirtle.

"It's the Squirtle Squad!" Ash cried.

Let the Games Begin!

Ash's Squirtle ran over to the Squirtle Squad. The team cheered up at the sight of their old friend. Squirtle slapped tails with each one of them.

"Pika, pika!" Pikachu greeted the Squirtle, too.

Ash, Misty, and Brock stepped up to the blue-haired police officer who had been directing the Squirtle Squad.

"Hi, Officer Jenny," Ash said. "Do you remember us?"

"How could I forget you three?" Officer

Jenny replied. "It was thanks to you that our gang of delinquent Squirtle became the best fire-fighting squad our town's ever seen."

Ash remembered the event well. When he met Squirtle, the Pokémon led the gang of troublemaking Squirtle. They terrorized their town. Ash had helped them see that doing good was a lot more rewarding than causing trouble. He and Squirtle had got along so well that Squirtle had decided to become one of Ash's Pokémon. Ash had relied on Squirtle ever since.

Aidan joined them. "Nice to meet you, Officer Jenny. I'm Aidan, captain of Team Wartortle. I look forward to our matchup."

"So do I, Captain," Jenny said. "Hey, would it be all right with you if the Squirtle Squad practiced with your Wartortle?"

"Sure," Aidan said. "Let's hit the target range."

Ash watched with interest as Team Wartortle and the Squirtle Squad lined up on the target range. Each team faced four round targets.

"The object of this exercise is to knock

down all four targets," Brock said. "Get ready, get set, go!"

Each Wartortle and Squirtle assaulted its target with a stream of water shot from its mouth. The Wartortle were spot-on in their aim. Each stream of water hit the target exactly in the center.

The Squirtle Squad wasn't having as much luck. Their water streams were aimed either too high or too low.

"Get it together, guys!" Officer Jenny encouraged them.

"Where's that Squirtle spirit?" Ash called out.

Ash's Squirtle watched the practice from Ash's side. Ash saw his Pokémon frown. Then Squirtle walked toward the Squirtle Squad.

"Where are you going?" Ash asked.

Squirtle didn't reply. It stomped on each Squirtle's tail. When it had their attention, Squirtle began barking orders.

"Squirtle! Squirtle Squirtle!"

The Squirtle Squad seemed to perk up. At Squirtle's command, they combined their four water streams into one powerful stream. They aimed the forceful stream at the first target.

Bang! The target snapped backward.

"That's it!" Jenny cried out happily. "Keep it up, guys!"

The Squirtle Squad took aim at the next target. On the other side, Team Wartortle had almost finished their task.

Bang! Team Wartortle knocked down the final target.

Bang! The Squirtle Squad finished right behind them.

"The Squirtle Squad really pulled together with Ash's Squirtle in charge," Misty remarked.

Brock nodded in agreement. "I guess it doesn't matter how long the old gang's been apart. The leader is still the leader."

Ash beamed proudly at his Squirtle. "Good job, Squirtle," he said.

Squirtle smiled. *"Squirtle Squirtle!"*

Soon it was time for the competiton. Aidan and Officer Jenny invited Ash, Misty, and Brock to watch from the team training area. Ash was glad for the opportunity. This way he could get an up-close view of the action.

Crowds of people filled the stadium. Ash and his friends stood on the side of the field, along with the other teams of firefighting Pokémon. Ash saw that two identical wooden houses had been set up on the field. He guessed that they might have something to do with the first test.

The stadium announcer's booming voice interrupted his thoughts.

"Welcome, ladies and gentlemen, to the Pokémon Fire-and-Rescue Grand Prix," the announcer said. "Teams of four Pokémon have come here today from far and wide to test their skills in red-hot competition. First up, let's welcome last year's second-place winners, the Golduck team. Today they're squaring off against the Squirtle Squad,

making their first appearance at the Grand Prix."

The crowd cheered.

"Okay, Squirtle Squad," Officer Jenny said. "Get out there and win this one!"

The four Squirtle ran out into the field and lined up in front of one of the wooden houses. Four Golduck lined up in front of the other. The Golduck had sleek blue bodies, webbed hands and feet, and yellow bills.

A booming sound rocked the stadium, and the two wooden houses suddenly burst into flames. A judge on the field raised a flag.

"The race is on!" shouted the announcer.

3

Robot Rampage

The Golduck quickly separated. Each Golduck started pelting one side of the house with water.

The Squirtle Squad ran toward the other house, but they tripped and fell and ended up in a tangled heap. When they finally got back on their feet, they formed a line in front of one side of the burning house. They began to shoot water at the raging flames.

But the Squirtle Squad looked nervous, and it showed in their attack. The water streams floundered in the air, and only sprinkles of water hit the flames.

The Golduck, on the other hand, were already making progress. Ash saw that they were beginning to douse the blaze.

"The Squirtle Squad is squirting hard, but they don't seem to have a plan of action," said the announcer. "Meanwhile, the Golduck team's coordinated offense is getting the job done. If someone doesn't light a fire under the Squirtle Squad, their efforts will go down the drain!"

Officer Jenny frowned. "Squirtle Squad, work together!" she shouted. "Aim at one place at a time."

Ash wasn't sure if the squad even heard Jenny. They continued their sloppy attack. He turned to his Squirtle. "They need you, Squirtle. They need their old leader."

Squirtle didn't hesitate. It ran up to the Squirtle Squad.

"Squirtle! Squirtle Squirtle!" Squirtle barked.

The Squirtle Squad immediately snapped to attention.

"*Squirtle Squirtle!*" Squirtle shouted.

They turned and faced the burning house again. This time, they combined their four streams of water into one powerful blast. The torrent quickly doused the flames on the side of house.

"And the soggy Squirtle Squad suddenly pours on the pressure!" said the announcer. "Talk about turnaround . . . talk about team-work!"

The Squirtle Squad zipped over to the

next side of the house. At Squirtle's command, they blasted the flames with water.

Across the field, the Golduck were almost done putting out the fire. Ash knew the squad would have to work superfast to pull this one off.

Finally, the Squirtle Squad reached the last side of the house.

"*Squirtle!*" cried Ash's Squirtle.

A tremendous wave of water came from the Squirtle Squad. Ash held his breath as the water enveloped the last of the orange flames.

The strategy worked! The last flame died out on the house. The fire on the other house died out, too, but the Golduck team was a split second too late.

"The match is ended. The Squirtle Squad wins!" boomed the announcer.

Officer Jenny gave Ash a big smile. "Your Squirtle is a natural-born leader," she said.

Officer Jenny, Ash, Brock, and Misty ran out to the field to congratulate the Squirtle Squad. Ash's Squirtle and the Squirtle Squad hugged one another and cheered.

Suddenly, a low rumbling sound filled the stadium. One of the wooden houses burst into flame once again.

"Hold it folks. Something's happening," said the announcer.

The ground next to the house began to shake. Ash watched, mouth open, as a giant red robot burst up from the ground and towered over the stadium. The bullet-shaped robot had a smooth, domed head made of clear glass. Its arms looked like giant hoses.

The lid of the dome popped open, and Ash saw three figures controlling the robot: Jessie, James, and their Pokémon, Meowth.

"Team Rocket!" Ash cried. The Pokémon thieves were always trying to steal his Pikachu — or any other Pokémon they could get their hands on.

Officer Jenny stepped toward the robot. "You're under arrest for disturbing a public event!"

Jessie laughed, tossing her long, red hair. "You'd better keep your cool, officer, because we're going to turn up the heat!"

Meowth cackled. "Speaking of heat, wait till you see the sparks fly when the burners get warmed up on this baby!"

"We hope you'll enjoy our new super-weapon," James added.

Meowth pressed a button, and the domed lid began to close.

"Fire up the Torcher Scorcher!" Meowth cried.

The robot's hoselike arms aimed at the fire-fighting Pokémon grouped on the field. Angry red flames exploded from the arms, aimed right for Ash and Pikachu.

The Pokémon reacted quickly. Aidan's Wartortle led a counter-assault, putting out the flames with powerful streams of water.

"Increase power!" Meowth cried.

This time, blazing fireballs burst out of the robot's arms. The other teams of firefighting Pokémon ran up to help the Wartortle.

A door in the robot's chest opened, and a bunch of nets swung down. In a flash, the nets swooped up the team of firefighting Pokémon — and Pikachu, too. Pikachu,

Team Wartortle, the Golduck, the Marill — they were all trapped in the net.

Squirtle and the Squirtle Squad were the only Pokémon to escape the nets. They charged toward the robot, but there was nothing they could do. Ash watched in horror as the net disappeared inside the robot, and the door slammed shut.

The robot stomped across the field in a crazy victory dance. Dangerous flames shot

out of its arms, narrowly missing the spectators in the stadium.

"This robot is on a red-hot rampage!" the announcer shouted.

Ash ran to his Squirtle. "The only way to save those Pokémon is if the Squirtle Squad can stop Team Rocket," said Ash. "And you've got to be their leader!"

Squirtle looked nervously at its four Squirtle friends. Ash knew what it was thinking: Can I really do this?

"You've got to do it, Squirtle," Ash said. "You're the only one that can."

Squirtle nodded. It ran to the Squirtle Squad and they huddled in a circle. When they broke the huddle, Ash saw that they were all wearing black sunglasses — the old trademark of the Squirtle Squad.

"All right!" Ash cheered. "The Squirtle Squad is back!"

4

Squirtle Squad to the Rescue

Squirtle and the Squirtle Squad ran up to the robot. Together they bombarded the robot with powerful water jets.

"Looks like it's time to put our foot down," said Meowth.

The robot lifted a giant metal leg. Ash cringed as the leg came down on top of Squirtle and the Squirtle Squad.

But the Squirtle were working as a smooth unit. They cleanly dodged out of the way of the stomping leg, never letting up on their water attack.

Meowth shook its paw. "We'll squash you like Bug Pokémon!"

The robot's legs tried to stomp the Squirtle team again and again. The Squirtle moved out of the way each time. They continued to bombard the robot with their Water Gun attack.

The powerful blasts caused the robot to teeter back and forth.

"It's losing its balance!" Ash cried.

Crash! The giant robot slammed onto the field.

Ash's Squirtle ran up to the robot's head. It smashed the glass of the dome. Then Squirtle blasted the robot's controls with a water stream. The controls popped and sizzled.

At the same time, the fire-fighting Pokémon escaped from the door in the belly of the robot. They ran out onto the field. Pikachu joined Ash's Squirtle.

Somehow, the robot managed to get back on its feet again. Ash couldn't believe it. But he knew the robot was weak — and he knew just what to do.

"Pikachu, Squirtle, go!" Ash yelled.

Squirtle and Pikachu stood side by side. Squirtle shot a stream of water at the robot. Pikachu added a bolt of electricity to the stream. The supercharged electricity lit up the robot like a neon sign. Then the robot took off like a rocket.

"Looks like Team Rocket's blasting off again!" cried Jessie, James, and Meowth.

A crowd in the stands cheered. Ash ran up to Pikachu and Squirtle. "Are you okay?" he asked them. They both nodded.

The announcer's voice drowned out the cheers. "Looks like our problem is solved. Welcome back to the Grand Prix!"

The teams of Pokémon were shaken, but no one wanted to quit. Ash relaxed and watched the competition continue. The Squirtle Squad continued in the semifinals. With Ash's Squirtle still leading them, they beat a team of Quagsire.

Team Wartortle made it to the semifinals, too. Ash cheered as they beat a team of Blastoise.

Finally, it was down to two teams.

"Team Wartortle will face the Squirtle Squad as each team races to retrieve a dummy from a burning building!" the announcer called out.

Ash wasn't sure who to root for. Aidan was his friend. But Squirtle and the Squirtle Squad were close to his heart. Secretly, he hoped they'd win.

Both teams gave it their all. The leader of Team Wartortle and Ash's Squirtle each ran into a different burning building. Sec-

onds later, Squirtle came out holding a dummy. The Wartortle leader came out right behind it.

Now the teams had to extinguish the fire. Team Wartortle and the Squirtle Squad pounded the flames with water. Ash held his breath. The race was close!

But the Squirtle Squad had an edge. After one powerful blast, the angry flames died.

"The competition is over!" shouted the announcer. "Officer Jenny's Squirtle Squad wins by a margin of one second."

Squirtle and the Squirtle Squad gave a cheer. The squad hoisted Squirtle on top of their shoulders.

At the sight of the happy Squirtle, a thought struck Ash. He walked up to Squirtle. The Pokémon climbed to the ground.

"The only way for the Squirtle Squad to be the best they can be is with you as their leader," Ash said. "They need you, Squirtle."

"Squirtle," Squirtle replied. Ash knew Squirtle was thinking the same thing.

Officer Jenny overheard. "Oh, thank you, Ash," she said. "With Squirtle back, we'll be the best fire-fighting force around."

Ash and the others stayed for a little while as the fire-and-rescue teams celebrated. But soon it was time to go. Ash let his Pokémon out of their Poké Balls so they could say good-bye to their friend.

"Squirtle, squirtle." Ash's Squirtle said farewell to Pikachu, Cyndaquil, and Chikorita. Then it walked up to Bulbasaur. Ash knew

that the Grass Pokémon was Squirtle's best friend. But Bulbasaur would not even look at Squirtle.

"*Squirtle?*" Squirtle asked.

Bulbasaur did not reply.

Squirtle sighed and turned around. But it didn't get far. A green vine snaked out of the plant bulb on Bulbasaur's back. Bulbasaur used the vine to shake hands with Squirtle. It smiled shyly at its friend.

Misty gave Squirtle a big hug. "We're going to miss you," she said. Ash could see tears in her green eyes.

Ash felt like crying, too. He held back his own tears as Squirtle hopped in the sidecar of Officer Jenny's motorcycle along with the Squirtle Squad.

"Don't forget, Squirtle," Ash said. "We'll always be friends, no matter what!"

"*Squirtle, Squirtle!*" agreed the Pokémon, and Officer Jenny sped off into the distance.

5

A Tricky Totodile

Ash knew he did the right thing by leaving Squirtle with Officer Jenny and the Squirtle Squad. But in the days that followed, Squirtle kept popping into his mind. Today was especially difficult. They had stopped at a riverbank, and all Ash could think about was Water Pokémon.

Misty couldn't stop talking about them, either.

"I'm right at home here by the water," Misty chattered. "You just watch. I'm going to catch a Water Pokémon today. I can feel it."

Brock yanked his fishing rod out of the water. The empty hook dangled in front of him. "I don't think any of us will catch anything today."

"Speak for yourself, Brock," Misty said. "I am going to be a Water Pokémon Master, and one day I'll — hey!"

Misty jumped back as drops of river water splashed her face. Ash looked up. A blue Pokémon had jumped out of the water and was standing on a rock in the river.

"It's a Totodile!" Ash cried. He recognized it from its big red eyes, its mouth filled with sharp teeth, and the ridges that ran down its back.

Totodile started to do a happy dance on the rock. Ash took out Dexter, his handheld computer, to find out more about it.

"Totodile, the Big Jaw Pokémon," Dexter said. "Its highly developed jaw has the strength to crush almost anything. It instinctively bites into whatever gets its attention."

"Cute *and* powerful," Ash said admiringly. "I'm gonna catch it."

"Oh, no you don't!" Misty said angrily. She quickly cast her fishing line at the To-

todile. The Pokémon swallowed the lure at the end of the line. Then it spit it back out and gave Misty a big wink.

"Hey!" Misty said.

"My turn," Ash said. "Pikachu, use Thunderbolt!"

Pikachu's red cheeks sizzled. It aimed a bolt of electricity at Totodile. The shock knocked Totodile backward. Ash didn't hesitate. He threw a Poké Ball at the Pokémon. Light flashed, and Totodile disappeared inside.

"No fair!" Misty complained.

But the Poké Ball began to wiggle. It cracked open, and Totodile appeared in a blaze of white light.

Brock shook his head. "It's not yours yet, Ash. It's out of the ball."

"It should be *mine,* anyway," Misty said. Before Ash could react, Misty threw one of her own Poké Balls at Totodile.

As the ball flew toward it, Totodile spun around once. Then it opened its mouth and aimed a blast of water at the Poké Ball. The ball shot back at Ash and Misty, knocking them both into the grass.

When Ash sat up, Totodile was gone. A splash of water kicked up from the river, as if Totodile were waving good-bye.

"It must be swimming upriver," Ash said. "I'm going to catch it. Come on, Pikachu."

"No, I'm going to catch it," Misty said. "Brock, take care of Togepi for me, will you?"

"But —" Brock tried to protest, but it was no use. Ash and Misty were on a mission. Before the day was over, one of them was going to catch Totodile!

6

Ash vs. Misty

"Pikachu! Use your sense of smell to find Totodile for me," Ash told the yellow Pokémon.

Pikachu scampered through the brush along the riverbank. Ash jogged behind it to keep up. To Ash's annoyance, Misty was right at his heels.

Finally, Pikachu stopped at a clearing. *"Pika!"* Pikachu pointed straight ahead.

Totodile lay stretched out in the grass, wearing a contented smile.

Ash took out a Poké Ball. "It won't get away from me this time."

"No way! Totodile is mine," Misty said angrily. She had pulled out a Poké Ball, too, but it didn't look like the one Ash held. It was white on the bottom and blue on the top. A red stripe decorated the blue half.

"Hey, that's the Poké Ball Kurt made for us," Ash said. Kurt, a friend of Professor Oak, was an expert on Poké Balls. He had crafted some special Poké Balls for Ash, Misty, and Brock during their recent visit.

"That's right. This is a Lure Ball, made especially for catching water Pokémon. Totodile won't wiggle out of this one!" Misty said confidently.

Ash had a Lure Ball, too. He quickly reached into his backpack and grabbed it.

Totodile still hadn't spotted them. Ash and Misty threw the Lure Balls at the same time. Totodile jumped up in the air. The two Lure Balls hit the Pokémon, knocking it behind a bush.

A light flashed behind the leafy bush. Ash

cheered. That meant a Poké Ball had caught Totodile!

He and Misty ran to the bush. Totodile was nowhere in sight. Two Lure Balls rested in the grass. One had a bright light shining from it. That meant Totodile was inside.

But whose Lure Ball was it?

Brock walked into the clearing carrying Togepi. "Hey, guys," he said. "Any luck?"

"I caught Totodile!" Misty said.

"No, I caught Totodile!" Ash countered.

They both reached down to grab the lit-up Lure Ball.

Brock quickly realized the problem. "You should have written your names on them."

"It doesn't matter," Ash said. He was getting angrier by the minute. "I know that ball is mine!"

"No, it's mine!" Misty said, her voice rising.

Ash and Misty clutched the Lure Ball. Neither would let go.

Brock stepped in and snatched the ball from them.

"I'll take that," he said. "There's only one way to settle this."

Ash and Misty looked at each other. "A Pokémon battle!"

Brock agreed to act as judge. They decided to use the clearing as a battle area. Ash didn't mind battling Misty at all, even if she was his friend. It was the best way to decide. Ash and Misty had started to battle once before, in Cerulean City. They had never finished. Ash was eager to find out if he could beat her. Getting the Totodile would be a bonus.

"Each of you will use a total of three Poké-mon in three one-on-one battles," Brock said.

That was just fine with Ash. "You think your Water Pokémon are great. But I've got the perfect Pokémon to beat them. Pikachu, of course!"

"*Pika!*" said Pikachu proudly. It stood in front of Ash, ready to start the battle.

Ash knew that Electric Pokémon like Pikachu always sizzled the competition when

Water Pokémon were involved. But Misty didn't look rattled.

"No problem. I have a secret weapon," she said, her green eyes gleaming.

"A secret weapon to beat Pikachu?" Ash didn't think Misty had any secrets that he didn't know about.

"I'll show you," Misty said. "Go, Togepi!"

"Togi!" The tiny Pokémon smiled happily and waddled past Misty.

Ash couldn't believe it. What could sweet little Togepi possibly do against Pikachu? Ash wasn't even sure if it had any attacks. Pikachu looked just as shocked.

"Let the first battle begin!" Brock cried.

Ash didn't know what to do. But if Misty wanted this battle, she'd get it. "Okay, Pikachu. Uh, try Thundershock."

"Pika?" Pikachu looked at Ash, horrified at the thought of shocking its little friend.

"Togepi, hug Pikachu!" Misty called out.

Togepi happily complied. It jumped into Pikachu's arms.

"Pikachu, do something," Ash pleaded. He couldn't lose to Togepi!

But Pikachu shook its head. It couldn't bear to attack Togepi. Ash couldn't blame it.

"Now use your Charm Attack, Togepi," Misty said.

Charm Attack? Ash had never heard of that before. Misty and Togepi must have been practicing that one.

Togepi hopped down from Pikachu's arms. It smiled and waved its arms. It looked to Ash like little pink hearts were floating through the air toward Pikachu.

Pikachu tried to run from the hearts, but it was a weak effort. It sank to the grass, shaking its head. Finally, Pikachu leaned back against a rock.

"Pikachu has lost the will to fight! The first battle goes to Misty," Brock said.

"I did it!" Misty cheered. "My plan to block Pikachu worked."

Ash had to admit that Misty had used a smart strategy. But the fight wasn't over yet. There were still two more battles. And he still had the advantage.

"Grass Pokémon are strong against Water Pokémon, too," Ash said. "Go, Chikorita!"

The pale-green Pokémon landed in the grass in front of Ash. On the other side of the clearing, Misty threw out a Poké Ball. Staryu, a Water Pokémon that looked like a five-pointed star, landed on two points. Staryu had a glittering red gem in the center of its body.

"You may have the advantage of Pokémon type," Misty said, "but I know how to fight any challenge with my Water Pokémon."

"Let the second battle begin!" Brock called out.

Chikorita started the battle with a Razor Leaf attack. Staryu jumped over the sharp leaves that Chikorita sent its way. Then Staryu countered by shooting a stream of stars out of its red jewel. The stars hit Chikorita, but the Grass Pokémon didn't back down.

"Chikorita, Tackle!" Ash shouted.

Chikorita obeyed quickly, slamming into Staryu's body. Staryu avoided another slam by digging straight down into the ground.

Chikorita stopped, waiting for Staryu's next move. How would the Water Pokémon get back to the surface?

"Use Water Gun!" Misty urged.

A geyser of water shot up from the ground. Staryu came shooting up behind it.

The water knocked Chikorita on its back. The Grass Pokémon jumped back on its feet. The little Pokémon looked angry.

"Chikorita, use Vine Whip!" Ash cried.

Two strong, green vines lashed out of the circles on Chikorita's neck. The vines wrapped around Staryu. Then Chikorita used them to slam Staryu against the ground again and again.

Staryu struggled to break free, but finally stopped moving.

"Staryu is unable to battle," Brock said. "Chikorita wins!"

"You did it, Chikorita," Ash said proudly. "If I win the next battle, I get Totodile."

"You won't win," Misty said, her mouth set in a determined line.

Ash and Misty called back Chikorita and Staryu. It was time to throw out the last two Pokémon.

Ash called on Bulbasaur. He'd caught the Grass Pokémon early in his journey, and

knew its abilities almost as well as he knew Pikachu's.

Misty chose Poliwag. The round, blue Pokémon stood about two feet tall. It had two short legs, no arms, and a long, flat tail. Its white belly was marked with a black spiral. It was strange-looking, but Ash knew it had some powerful attacks.

"Begin the battle!" Brock yelled.

Ash and Misty started out with their Pokémon's strongest attacks. Bulbasaur lashed at Poliwag with its vines. Poliwag smacked Bulbasaur with its strong tail.

Ash tried a Razor Leaf Attack next. The sharp leaves battered Poliwag. The Water Pokémon looked shaken.

"Don't give up, Poliwag," Misty said. "Water Gun!"

A strong blast of water poured from Poliwag's mouth, dousing Bulbasaur. But the Grass Pokémon stayed focused. Another round of Razor Leaves flew out of the bulb on its back.

Once again, the leaves battered Poliwag.

Weakened from the first attack, Poliwag started to sway.

"Poliwag!" Misty cried.

But Poliwag toppled over into the grass.

"We did it!" Ash cheered.

"That decides it," Brock said. "This battle, in a two to one victory, goes to . . ."

"Wait!" Misty cried.

A glowing white light bathed Poliwag's body. Ash had seen that happen a few times before. It could only mean one thing.

"Poliwag's evolving!" Misty said happily.

Poliwhirl vs. Bulbasaur

The white light swirled around Poliwag's body. Then the light flashed, and a new Pokémon stood in Poliwag's place.

In its evolved form, Poliwag lost its tail, but gained two strong arms. Poliwhirl looked a lot tougher, too.

Ash took out Dexter.

"Poliwhirl, the Tadpole Pokémon," said the computer. "With highly developed muscles, this Pokémon can move ably on land, but it is more agile in water."

"Because Poliwag evolved, this battle can continue," Brock said.

"Bulbasaur can take whatever you throw at it," Ash told Misty. "Bulbasaur, Tackle!"

"Poliwhirl, Body Slam!" Misty said.

Ash knew she was relying on Poliwhirl's increased strength to take down Bulbasaur. It was a good instinct. Poliwhirl launched into Bulbasaur, pinning the Grass Pokémon to the ground.

It wasn't easy, but Bulbasaur broke away. It fought back with a stream of Razor Leaves. But this time, the attack didn't seem to phase the Pokémon.

Ash wanted to win so bad he could taste it. And Bulbasaur had one attack that could take down almost any Pokémon.

"Bulbasaur, use Solar Beam!" Ash cried.

Bulbasaur opened the plant bulb on its back and began to draw in sunlight for the attack.

Misty looked concerned for a second, but then she brightened. "Poliwhirl, attack Bulbasaur while it's getting energy. Use Bubble Attack!"

Poliwhirl began to shoot powerful bubbles from its mouth. The bubbles collided with Bulbasaur at a rapid speed.

Ash held his breath. Bulbasaur looked weak. Would it make it?

Just in time, Ash saw Bulbasaur's plant bulb close. It had gathered the sunlight it needed.

"Bulbasaur, launch Solar Beam!" Ash shouted.

Ash saw Misty cringe as a golden beam of light escaped from Bulbasaur's plant bulb. The light bombarded Poliwhirl.

The Water Pokémon didn't stand a chance. It collapsed in a heap.

Misty ran to her Pokémon. "Are you okay?"

"Poliwhirl," replied the Pokémon weakly.

Misty hugged it. "Thank you for evolving just to help me win."

"And now it's official," Brock said. "Victory goes to Ash!"

"We did it!" Ash picked up Bulbasaur. Pikachu danced happily at his feet.

But before Ash could get too carried away, confetti dropped from the sky.

"Huh?" Ash wondered. Since when did confetti fall in the woods?

Two people and one very short person wearing red robes and white masks burst from the bushes.

"We're here to help you celebrate!" they said.

Things were getting weirder and weirder. And there was something strangely familiar about them . . .

As the people danced around, the mask on the short person slipped off. Ash saw that it wasn't a person at all. It was a Pokémon — Meowth!

"Team Rocket!" Ash cried.

Jessie, James, and Meowth threw off their disguises.

"We couldn't help noticing your battle," Jessie said.

"And now that you're all worn out, we'll take Pikachu off your hands," Meowth said.

Ash grabbed the Lure Ball from Brock. "Not so fast," he said. "We have a new friend. Go, Totodile!"

Totodile burst from the ball. Without hesitation, it jumped up and chomped down on Jessie's long hair.

"Get off me, you little beast!" Jessie shrieked. She swung her hair, sending Totodile flying.

Jessie and James each threw out a Poké Ball.

"Go, Arbok!" Jessie cried, as the purple Cobra Pokémon appeared.

"Go, Weezing!" yelled James. Weezing, a purple Pokémon with two heads, moaned as it floated out of the ball.

Ash knew just how to take down these guys. "Totodile, Bite Arbok!"

Totodile chomped down on Arbok's tail. At Ash's command, it swung Arbok like a baseball bat, knocking over Jessie, James, and Meowth. Totodile did a happy dance as its opponent went down.

But Team Rocket wasn't finished yet.

"Weezing, Sludge Attack!" James shouted.

Brown sludge oozed from Weezing's body. Totodile kept on dancing, dodging the attack with its quick footwork.

Then Totodile jumped on top of Weezing. It scratched at the Pokémon with its claws.

Weezing couldn't take it. It fell on top of Arbok and the rest of Team Rocket.

"Finish up with Water Gun!" Ash told Totodile.

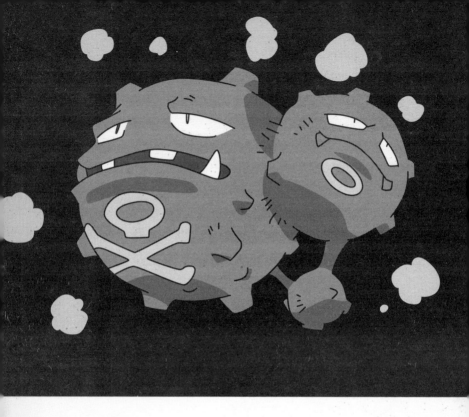

A wild wave of water shot from Totodile's mouth, sending Team Rocket careening into the sky.

"Looks like Team Rocket's blasting off again!" they shouted.

Totodile did another happy dance.

"We've certainly added an interesting member to our team," Brock remarked.

Misty approached Ash. "You handled that

Totodile really well," she said, smiling. "You've become a really strong trainer. And I guess since we're friends, it doesn't matter who keeps Totodile, right?"

Ash smiled back, relieved that he and Misty were still friends.

"Thanks, Misty," he said. Then Ash reached down and hoisted Totodile onto his shoulders.

"I caught a Totodile!" he said proudly.

The Lovely Azumarill

"Wow, look at Totodile go!" Misty said.

In the days since Ash had first caught Totodile, he was constantly amazed at the things his new Pokémon could do. Today they had camped out by a lake. Totodile was playing in the water with some of Misty's Water Pokémon: Staryu, Goldeen, and Psyduck. Staryu swam under the surface. Graceful Goldeen flipped its frilly orange and white fins. Psyduck couldn't swim. It stood on the shore and flapped its wings.

Totodile, meanwhile, was having a blast.

It showed off for Ash and the others, swimming in circles and floating on its back. Then it found three Magikarp swimming in the water. It grabbed the fish Pokémon and started juggling them in a geyser of water it shot from its mouth.

"That's my Totodile for you," Ash said proudly. Finding Totodile was the best thing that could have happened. He still missed Squirtle, but Totodile helped him take his mind off it.

Ash leaned back in the grass and closed his eyes. The smell of Brock's delicious cooking wafted through the air. Battling Pokémon was fun, but every Pokémon trainer needed to relax once in a while.

Ash's peace didn't last long. His eyes flew open at the sound of Misty's cry.

"Hey look — it's a Golduck!" Misty said.

Ash sat up and turned around. A Golduck was walking through the woods behind them. It looked almost like it was searching for something.

Misty held out a Poké Ball. "I'm not going to waste this chance. I'm going to catch it!"

Ash put an arm out to stop her. "Wait, Misty. That is no ordinary Golduck."

At Ash's words, a girl Brock's age came through the trees. A blue bow was tied in her long red hair. A brown, feathered Pidgey sat on her shoulder.

Brock put down his cooking spoon and ran toward the girl. Ash heard Misty groan. Brock tried to flirt with every girl they met.

"You look like you need help," Brock said. "And I am just the one to help you. My name's

Brock. That's B for Blastoise, R for Rapidash, O for Onyx, C for Cloyster, and K for Kadabra. I'm as powerful as a Blastoise, graceful as a Rapidash, strong as an Onyx . . ."

The girl looked a little taken aback. "I'm Beverly," she said, interrupting him.

"Beverly," Brock said. "That's B, like the lovely Butterfree . . ."

Ash came to Beverly's rescue. "Is this your Golduck?" he asked her.

"Yes," Beverly said, looking relieved. "We're in town with the Pokémon Circus. Our Azumarill is missing, and we're trying to find it."

"What's an Azumarill?" Ash asked. He took out Dexter.

"Azumarill," Dexter said. "The Aquarabbit Pokémon is the evolved form of Marill. It uses its highly developed ears to hear sounds, even under strong water currents."

Just then, a blue Pokémon ran out of the bushes. It had long, pointy ears. White spots decorated its round body.

"Azumarill!" Beverly said happily.

The Azumarill ran up to Beverly and hid behind her legs. It looked as though it was hiding from something.

Then Ash saw what it was. Totodile burst through the bushes next. It stopped in front of Beverly.

Totodile danced around, never taking its eyes off of Azumarill. Heart-shaped bubbles floated out of its mouth.

"Totodile? What are you doing?" Ash asked.

Misty leaned over and whispered in Ash's ear. "I think Totodile has a crush on Azumarill!"

9

T°t°dile in L°Ve

"Ladies and gentlemen, boys and girls, welcome to the Pokémon Circus!"

Ash and his friends sat in the front row inside the circus tent. Pikachu and Totodile sat by his side. Ash held his breath as the ringmaster walked out of the ring.

Beverly was so happy at finding Azumarill that she had invited them all to see the circus. The idea of a troupe of traveling, performing Pokémon intrigued Ash. He couldn't wait to see what was in store.

Beverly came out first, dressed in a tuxedo and top hat. She performed a magic act with a blue Marill as her assistant. Beverly put the Marill in the top hat, then put the top hat on her head. When she took off the hat, a Pidgey flew out!

Ash clapped along with the crowd. Beverly performed a few more magic tricks, then left the ring.

The ringmaster's voice rang out. "Now get ready for our beautiful star. It's time for Azumarill's spectacular water show!"

A curtain rose in the ring to reveal Azumarill standing on a round platform studded with stars. A basket of colorful balls was nearby.

Azumarill shot water out of its mouth. The waves formed a beautiful waterfall in the air. Azumarill tossed up colored balls until they all danced on the bubbling streams.

"That's great," said Misty. "It really is the star of the show."

Totodile could not take its eyes off Azumarill. Before Ash could stop it, Totodile jumped out of its seat and ran into the circus ring.

"Totodile!" Totodile added its own water stream to Azumarill's.

Azumarill scowled, but the audience thought Totodile was funny. Some of them began to throw fruit at Totodile to see if it could juggle.

Totodile jumped toward the fruit, not miss-

ing a beat. Soon a banana, orange, and apple were suspended in Totodile's water stream.

That was too much for Azumarill. The Pokémon stormed out of the ring. The colored balls tumbled back onto the platform.

"Totodile!" Ash's Pokémon did not like to see Azumarill unhappy. It stopped its water stream. Ash and Pikachu ran into the ring to catch the falling fruit. The crowd applauded as Ash caught an apple in one hand and a banana in another. Pikachu caught an apple using the top of its head.

"Uh, thank you," Ash said.

After the show, Ash found Beverly so he could apologize.

"It's okay," Beverly said. "The audience loved it. Besides, Azumarill has been acting strangely for a while now. I'm not sure what's wrong with her."

Ash felt better. He and the others went back to their campsite, where Ash slept soundly in his sleeping bag. He could talk to Totodile in the morning.

But when Ash woke up, Totodile was

nowhere to be seen. And Brock wasn't cooking breakfast, as usual.

"I wonder where they could be?" Ash said.

"Nobody knows more about falling in love than I do," Brock told Totodile. The older boy had decided to help the Pokémon with his crush on Azumarill. They had traced Azumarill to a shady spot under a tree. Brock talked in hushed tones so the Pokémon couldn't hear them.

Brock handed Totodile a jar of his special Pokémon food. "The way to a girl's heart is lots of presents," Brock said. "If you give this to Azumarill, it's sure to fall for you."

Totodile hesitantly took the jar from Brock. After upsetting Azumarill at the circus, it was afraid of making another wrong move.

"Do it, Totodile," Brock said. "You owe it to yourself to try."

Totodile nodded its head. It shyly walked toward Azumarill.

"Totodile?" Totodile held out the jar of food.

"Azu!" Azumarill jumped up and started to walk away from Totodile. It wasn't interested in the food at all.

"Totodile!" Totodile ran after the blue Pokémon.

Brock watched the pair from behind the bush. He didn't expect that Totodile would

win Azumarill easily. But he also didn't expect what he saw next.

A net dropped out of the sky and scooped up Azumarill.

Brock looked up. The net was dangling from Team Rocket's balloon!

The balloon began to rise into the air.

Brock and Totodile ran toward the balloon. "Don't worry, Azumarill! We'll save you!" Brock screamed.

10

Search for the Stolen Pokémon

Ash heard Brock's screams. He, Misty, and Pikachu took off in the direction of his voice, crashing through the bushes as they ran.

Soon Ash spotted the balloon rising above the trees. Ash quickly caught up to Brock and Totodile.

"They've got Azumarill," Brock explained, trying to catch his breath.

"This talented Pokémon will make us lots of cash," James called down from the balloon. Weezing floated by his side. "Azumarill is coming with us."

"We won't let you!" Ash cried. He turned to Pikachu. "Pikachu, use Thunderbolt!"

The balloon was rising higher and higher. Pikachu jumped up to launch the attack.

Up in the balloon basket, Meowth grinned. "Just what we were waiting for," purred the Pokémon. Then it launched a rope over the side of the balloon. A red ball hung from the end of the rope.

The ball met Pikachu in midair. Then it opened up, transforming into a silver cage. The cage scooped up Pikachu, then snapped tightly shut.

"Pikachu!" Ash cried. He reached for another Poké Ball. He had to rescue his friend!

James didn't give him a chance. "Weezing, Smoke Screen!" James called.

The purple Poison Pokémon belched, and thick black smoke floated down from the balloon. Ash's eyes watered as the smoke stung his eyes. He couldn't see a thing.

When the smoke cleared, Ash saw that the

balloon had cleared the woods and now floated halfway across the lake. Team Rocket was out of reach.

"Totodile!" The Water Pokémon leaped into the lake without hesitation and began to swim after the balloon.

Ash nearly jumped in after it, but he knew he couldn't catch up with the balloon that way.

"Come back, Totodile!" he called out. But the small Pokémon ignored Ash, determined to save his friends.

Ash turned to Brock and Misty. "I won't give up," he said.

"We don't have to," Brock replied. "I'm sure those thieves are on the other side of the lake. We can catch up with them. But first let's get Beverly and tell her what's happened."

Ash nodded. "Let's go!"

It didn't take long to find Beverly, and soon they made their way around the lake on foot. Beverly's Pidgey sat on her shoulder, and her Golduck led the way through the trees. Ash fought off a sick, angry feeling with each step. Team Rocket had often tried to steal Pikachu, but they rarely succeeded. And now he might never see Pikachu again. To make matters worse, he didn't even know where Totodile was. For all he knew, Team Rocket had Totodile, too.

"Azumarill! Pikachu! Totodile!" Misty and Brock called out to the Pokémon again and again. But there was never an answer.

Then Beverly had an idea. "Pidgey, go find the balloon for us," she told it.

Pidgey cooed, then flew off over the trees.

They walked a few minutes more. Ash hoped Pidgey would return with some news. Then, suddenly, he saw a flash of white above the green treetops.

"It's Team Rocket's balloon!" Ash cried. He charged toward it at top speed.

As he watched the balloon, he could see Pidgey flying around it. Behind him, he heard Beverly yell, "Pidgey, stop that balloon!"

"Pidgey!" The tiny bird Pokémon dove at the balloon, ripping into it with its sharp beak. Hot air rushed out from the hole.

Ash ran out into a clearing. The damaged

balloon teetered overhead. Brock, Misty, and Beverly came to a stop behind Ash.

With no more air to hold it up, the balloon plunged to the ground.

"Looks like our plan is busted!" Meowth screamed.

Crash! The balloon basket slammed into the grass. Two cages flew out.

Ash leaped forward and caught one of the cages. To his relief, he saw Pikachu was inside. Brock caught the other cage, which held Totodile.

Ash put down Pikachu's cage and turned to face Team Rocket.

"You won't get away with this," he told them. "You've gone too far."

"You'll never stop us," Jessie said.

Meowth held up a third cage. "You won't try anything," said the Pokémon. "Because we've still got Azumarill!"

11

Azumarill's Secret

Ash reached for a Poké Ball, but Beverly's Golduck was quicker. It ran up toward the balloon.

"What are you doing, Golduck?" Beverly called out nervously.

The sight of the feathered Pokémon didn't phase Team Rocket. Jessie and James each threw out a Poké Ball.

"Go, Arbok!" cried Jessie.

"Go, Weezing!" James shouted.

The Pokémon burst from their balls, but

Golduck didn't wait for them to attack. It blasted them both with a powerful torrent of water.

At the same time, Ash threw out Bulbasaur. "Use Razor Leaf," he told his Pokémon.

Sharp leaves flew out of Bulbasaur's plant bulb, slicing through the bars of the cages that held Pikachu and Totodile. The two Pokémon ran out, ready to join the fight.

Totodile sprang into action, blasting Jessie, James, and Meowth with a ferocious Water Gun attack. Meowth dropped Azumarill's cage, and Bulbasaur quickly grabbed it with its long green vines. Once Azumarill was safe, Pikachu finished them off with a powerful Thundershock.

Team Rocket glowed with electricity as Pikachu's attack coursed through them.

Bam! Ash shielded his face from the explosion as Team Rocket went careening off into the distance.

"Looks like Team Rocket's blasting off again!" they screamed.

Ash gave Bulbasaur one last command. "Use Razor Leaf to free Azumarill!"

Bulbasaur complied, and Azumarill ran out of the cage. A hopeful grin spread across Totodile's face. Was Azumarill running toward Totodile?

For a second, even Ash thought Totodile had won its quest for Azumarill's love. Totodile closed its eyes, waiting . . .

. . . and Azumarill ran past it, straight into the arms of Golduck!

"What happened?" Ash wondered.

"Simple," Misty said. "Azumarill has a crush on Golduck."

Beverly knelt down in front of Azumarill. "Is this why you've been acting so strange and sad?" she asked.

Azumarill nodded. Then it looked up and smiled at Golduck. Golduck smiled back.

Only Totodile looked miserable. The poor Pokémon couldn't even look at Azumarill and Golduck.

"I know just how you feel," Brock told Totodile.

Soon they began the long walk back to their campsite. Pikachu rode on Ash's shoulders. Ash felt great to have his Pokémon back again.

Totodile lagged behind them, sighing as it walked.

"Don't worry," Misty told Ash. "I'm sure Totodile will get over it soon."

Suddenly, Brock stopped. "Hey, what's that?"

A Quagsire sat on a rock along the river. The sleek blue Pokémon had a smooth, round head and a long, flat tail. A pretty red bow decorated its head.

Totodile stopped in its tracks. Then it smiled. It ran over to the Quagsire. It began to dance and show off.

Misty groaned. "That Totodile never gives up. It reminds me of you, Brock."

Ash grinned. "I think Totodile takes after me," he said.

"What do you mean?" Misty asked.

"Totodile won't give up on love. And I

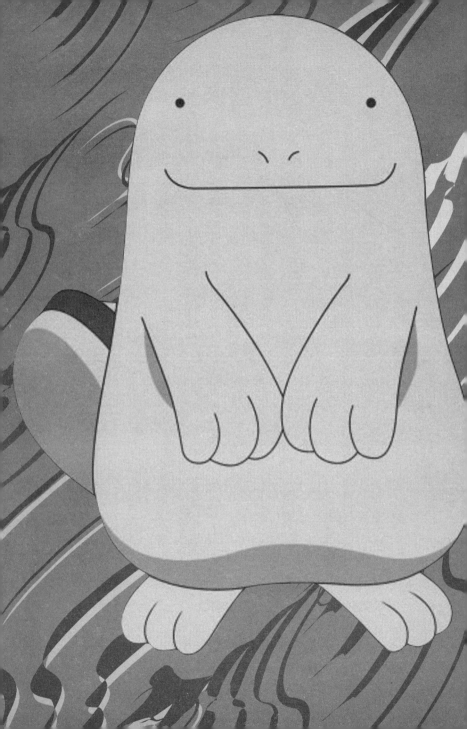

won't give up on my dream of becoming a Pokémon Master," Ash said.

Misty and Brock laughed.

Ash turned around and called to Totodile.

"Let's go, Totodile," Ash said. "The rest of the Johto Region is waiting for us!"

About the Author

Tracy West has been writing books for more than ten years. When she's not playing the blue version of the Pokémon game (she started with a Squirtle), she enjoys reading comic books, watching cartoons, and taking long walks in the woods (looking for wild Pokémon). She lives in a small town in New York with her family and pets.

POKéMON

GOTTA READ 'EM ALL!™